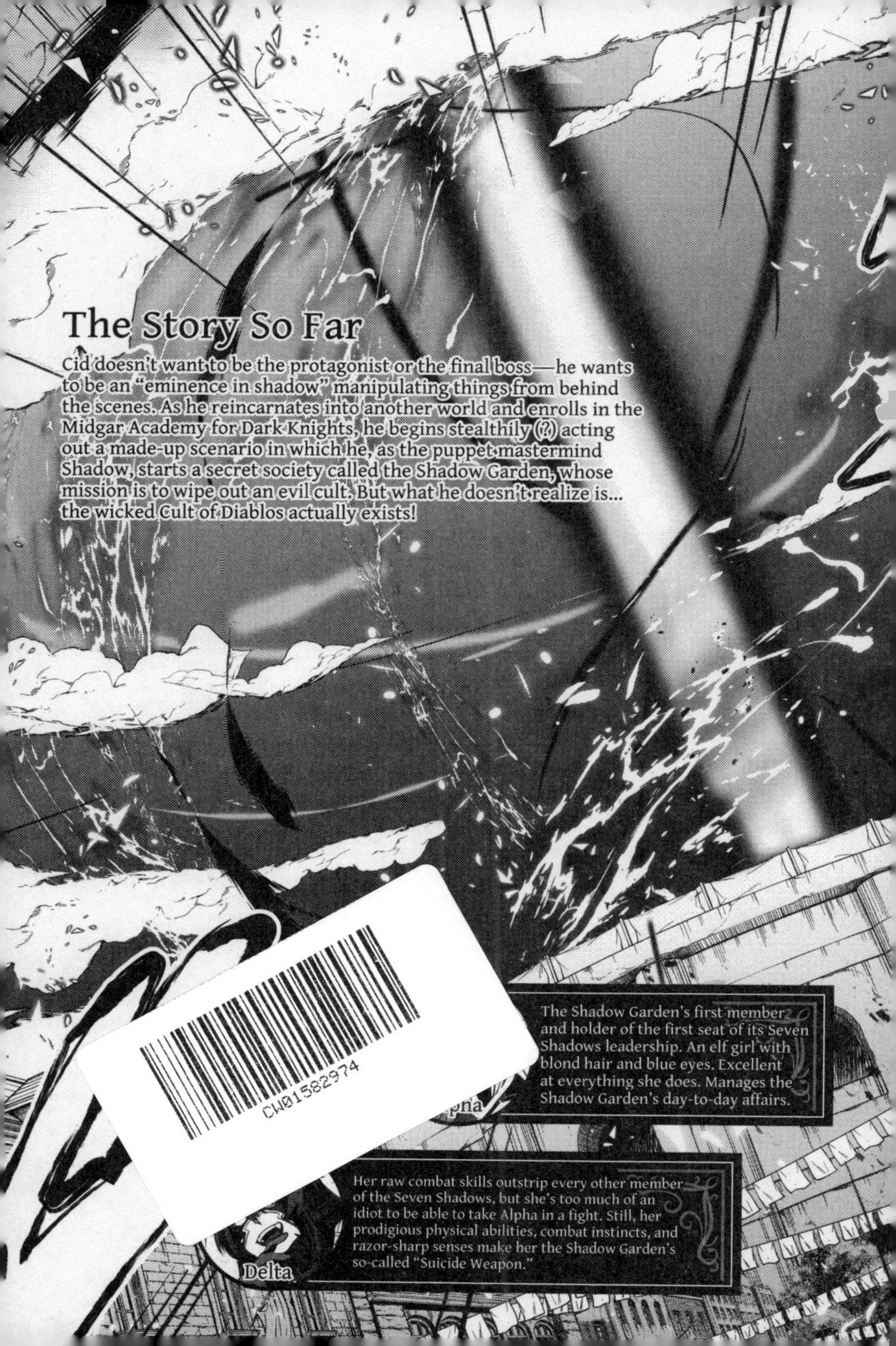

The Story So Far

Cid doesn't want to be the protagonist or the final boss—he wants to be an "eminence in shadow" manipulating things from behind the scenes. As he reincarnates into another world and enrolls in the Midgar Academy for Dark Knights, he begins stealthily (?) acting out a made-up scenario in which he, as the puppet mastermind Shadow, starts a secret society called the Shadow Garden, whose mission is to wipe out an evil cult. But what he doesn't realize is... the wicked Cult of Diablos actually exists!

[Al]pha

The Shadow Garden's first member and holder of the first seat of its Seven Shadows leadership. An elf girl with blond hair and blue eyes. Excellent at everything she does. Manages the Shadow Garden's day-to-day affairs.

Delta

Her raw combat skills outstrip every other member of the Seven Shadows, but she's too much of an idiot to be able to take Alpha in a fight. Still, her prodigious physical abilities, combat instincts, and razor-sharp senses make her the Shadow Garden's so-called "Suicide Weapon."

[CONTENTS]

The Eminence in Shadow

10

Art Anri Sakano

Original Story Daisuke Aizawa

Character Design Touzai

NEVER LOSE SIGHT...
GOO (RRRMB)
...OF WHO YOUR REAL ENEMY IS.
Cid Kagenou
During his mad training to become an eminence in shadow, an unfortunate accident led to him being reincarnated into the Midgar Kingdom. After training (again) to become an eminence in shadow in his new world, he mastered an ultimate hidden technique more powerful than a nuke. Founded the Shadow Garden so he could live out his shadowbroker fantasies.
Rose Oriana
An exchange student from a land of art and culture called the Oriana Kingdom, and the daughter of King Oriana. On top of that, she's the student council president. Her rapier work is beautiful, and her appreciation for the arts is second to none. Was recently saved by Cid due to his "burning passion" for her (or so she believes).
Yukime
The Spirit Fox who rules the White Tower and controls the Lawless City's pleasure district. She's sharp as a tack and moves like a dancer when she fights with her iron fans. Shadow saved some of her working girls when the ghouls went on their rampage.

PLEASE, SHADOW.
I DON'T UNDER-STAND.
Episode.38
TELL ME, WHY!?
WHY ARE YOU DOING THIS!!?
...BECAUSE IT WAS THE BEST OPTION.
THAT'S ALL I'LL SAY UNTIL THIS IS OVER.

I'M JOHN SMITH NOW.
I'VE ALREADY ABANDONED...
...THE NAME OF SHADOW.
......
AND WHERE'S DELTA...?
WHAT DID YOU DO TO HER?
GU (CLENCH)
......
DELTA... LEFT ON A LONG JOURNEY.

THAT DOESN'T ...
...TELL ME ANY-THING!!!
ZA (SLICE)
I'M DUMB, SO I DON'T GET THE WAY YOU THINK!
HYU (SWIPP)
I'M WEAK, SO I'M NOT CAPABLE OF THE THINGS YOU ARE!!
BA (WSHH)

BUT I WANT TO UNDER-STAND AND SUPPORT YOU IN SPITE OF THAT!!
YOU SAVED US, AND I WANT TO BE THERE FOR YOU!!!
BUT YOU ALWAYS JUST RUSH OFF AHEAD ON YOUR OWN...
...AND LEAVE US STARING POWER-LESSLY AT YOUR BACK!!

SU (SHFF)
...SEE?
I CAN NEVER REACH YOU.
ARE YOU SAYING...
...YOU DON'T NEED ME ANYMORE?
I'M DOING WHAT MUST BE DONE.
I SEE...

WELL, I'M THROUGH...
...WITH BEING A BURDEN.
GOO (RRRMB)
FU (SHFF)
!!?

KIN
(SHNNG)
HYUN
(SWOOSH)

SAAA (WHOOSH)
BUSHU (THWICK)
IS THIS...
ZA (SLICE)
ZA
...RED MIST ...!?
ZA
ZASHU (SLASH)
THAT'S RIGHT...WE STUDIED THE VAMPIRE BLOOD WE GOT FROM THE LAWLESS CITY AND PUT IT TO USE.
TURNING TO MIST LETS ME SENSE THE POSITION AND MOVEMENTS OF YOUR THREADS...
...AND ATTACK YOU FROM ANY RANGE.
ZASHU

I TOLD YOU, I'M NOT JUST SOME BURDEN ANYMORE.
SO PLEASE, JUST—
FASCI-NATING.
BUT YOU'VE GOT ONE PROB-LEM.
ZU (VRRP)
ZU
ZU

IF I BLOW IT ALL AWAY...
...THERE'S NOTHING YOU CAN DO.
GOO (RRRMB)

ZAAAAAA
(WHOOSH)
IF YOU'D STAYED IN MISTFORM, YOU'D HAVE GOTTEN BLOWN RIGHT INTO THE STRATO-SPHERE.
YOU MADE THE RIGHT CALL.

YOU'VE GROWN STRONG.
TON (THMP)

PLEASE
...
DON'T LEAVE ME...
ARE YOU REALLY
...
...GOING TO TURN YOUR BACK ON ME AGAIN...?

WELL, WELL, WELL.
OUR PLAN IS FINALLY REACHING ITS FINALE.
WE'VE SUCCESSFULLY LIQUIDATED ALL OUR COUNTERFEITS.
I WOULD SAY WE'VE EARNED PLENTY FOR OURSELVES, WOULDN'T YOU?
INDEED WE HAVE... EXCELLENT WORK.
THE PRICE OF GOODS HAS STARTED RISING DUE TO THE INFLUX OF CURRENCY INTO THE SYSTEM.
BY MY ESTIMATE, THE INFLATION RATE WILL, UH...GO UP BY LOTS.

I SEE YOU'VE BEEN KEEPING ON TOP OF YOUR INTEL GATHERING. IMPRESSIVE AS ALWAYS, MR. JOHN.
YET AGAIN, I FIND MYSELF REMINDED OF HOW FORTU-NATE I WAS TO FORM THIS PARTNERSHIP.
THE PLAN NEVER WOULD HAVE WORKED WERE IT NOT FOR YOUR EFFORTS.
NOW, ALL WE HAVE LEFT TO DO IS TAKE THE GENUINE BILLS WE SQUIR-RELED AWAY AND EXCHANGE THEM AT THE MCA.
THEY NO LONGER HAVE ENOUGH GOLD IN THEIR RESERVES...
...TO CONVERT THE AMOUNT OF CASH WE HAVE ON HAND.
AND SO BEGINS THE CREDIT COLLAPSE.

I SHALL EXCHANGE THE BILLS IN PERSON.
THE PLAN IS MEANINGLESS IF I FAIL TO DELIVER THE DEATH BLOW MYSELF.
YOU'RE STILL AFTER REVENGE, THEN?
I AM.
BEFORE WE CARRY OUT THE FINAL STEP...
...ALLOW ME TO EXPLAIN WHY I CARE SO DEEPLY.
I WAS NOT AS POWERFUL THEN AS I AM NOW.
IT ALL HAPPENED BUT A FEW YEARS AGO...

I LIVED IN A SMALL SPIRIT FOX VILLAGE...
...AND WORKED AS A HUNTER ALONGSIDE MY MOTHER.
LOOK, MOTHER!
TA
TA (DASH)
OUR DRIED MEAT STORES ARE GROWING LOW.
I SHOULD GO OUT HUNTING AGAIN BEFORE WINTER COMES.
LEAVE THE HUNTING TO US ADULTS, HONEY.
BUT WHY!? I'M STRONG AND GROWN-UP TOO!!
WELL, IT'S NO WONDER YOU'RE STRONG, YUKIME.
YOUR MOM HERE HAS THREE WHOLE TAILS, AFTER ALL.

OUR RIVAL CLANS MIGHT STAGE ANOTHER ATTACK ON US.
BUT THAT'S WHY IT'S SO IMPORTANT YOU STAY HERE AND PROTECT THE VILLAGE.
AT THE TIME, CONFLICT BETWEEN THERIANTHROPES RAGED WITHOUT END.
THE POWERFUL CLANS WERE CONSTANTLY INVADING THEIR NEIGHBORS IN AN ATTEMPT TO WREST POWER FROM EACH OTHER.
AND THAT NIGHT, WHEN THE ADULTS WERE OUT HUNTING, WAS NO DIFFERENT...
EVERYONE, HIDE!!
WAAA (CLAMOR)
WE'RE UNDER ATTACK!!!
AA (SCREAM)

HEH-HEH. LOOK AT WHAT WE'VE GOT HERE.
I THINK I'LL TAKE YOU BACK WITH ME AS A TROPHY.
C'MERE, YOU!!
NO!!
LET GO OF ME!!
GUI (YANK)
OW! DAMN IT!!
GABU (CHOMP)
YOU LITTLE SHIT ...!!!

GIN (WHAM)
ARE YOU OKAY?
NAME'S GETTAN.
DON'T WORRY, I'M ON YOUR SIDE.

HE WAS A DILIGENT YOUNG MAN, AND HE WORKED HARD ON BEHALF OF THE VILLAGE.
THE GREAT WOLF CLAN HAD COME TO BACK US UP, AND HE WAS THE SON OF ITS CHIEF.
IT DIDN'T TAKE LONG FOR US TO BECOME FAST FRIENDS.
SHORTLY THEREAFTER, IT WAS DECIDED THAT IN ORDER TO FURTHER STRENGTHEN OUR ALLIANCE...
...I, AS THE DAUGHTER OF THE SPIRIT FOX CLAN'S THREE-TAILS...
...AND GETTAN, AS THE GREAT WOLF CLAN'S STRONGEST WARRIOR, WERE TO BE ENGAGED.
NOBODY HAD ANY OBJECTIONS.
WE HAD EVERYONE'S BLESSING, AND BY ALL RIGHTS, OUR WEDDING WAS GOING TO BE A HAPPY ONE...

WAAAAA (SCREAM)
DAMN IT...
DAMN IT ALL!!
IF ONLY I WERE STRONGER...
THEN I COULD HAVE PROTECTED THEM...I COULD HAVE SAVED THE VILLAGE!!
I'M SO SORRY.
IT TOOK EVERYTHING I HAD JUST TO GET YOU OUT OF THERE...!!

THE ONLY ONES TO BLAME HERE ARE THE BIGGER CLANS AND THEIR HUGE ARMY.
THERE'S NOTHING TO APOLO-GIZE FOR, GETTAN.
THERE'S NO WAY YOU COULD HAVE DEFEATED A FORCE THE SIZE OF—
SHUT UP!!
IF I WERE STRONGER, I WOULDN'T HAVE GOTTEN STOLEN FROM!!!
I WOULD HAVE BEEN ABLE TO PROTECT THEM!!
BIKU (TWITCH)
GETTAN ...?
YORO (STAGGER)
...SORRY.
BUT YOU HAVE TO UNDERSTAND, YUKIME.
THE FACT OF THE MATTER IS, WE WERE TOO WEAK.

THAT'S WHY I MADE MY PROPOSAL TO THE OTHERS.
I TOLD THEM THAT IF WE TOOK THESE PILLS, WE COULD OBTAIN IMMENSE POWER!!
ALL WE HAD TO DO WAS ACCEPT THE CULT'S PROTECTION...
...AND NOBODY WOULD EVER BE ABLE TO BEAT US AGAIN!!!
...WHAT?
PILLS ...?
THE CULT ...?
WHAT ARE YOU TALKING ABOUT ...?
...IT'S ALL THAT WOMAN'S FAULT.

AS SOON AS SHE REJECTED THE PILLS...
...EVERY-ONE ELSE FOLLOWED HER LEAD!!
BUT DON'T WORRY.
THAT'S NEVER GOING TO HAPPEN AGAIN.
AFTER ALL, I JUST KILLED HER!!!
I USED THE CHAOS AS COVER TO LOP OFF HER HEAD!!!
YOU'RE A SMART COOKIE...
...SO YOU GET WHY I HAD TO DO IT, RIGHT!?
THIS WAS THE ONLY WAY FOR ME TO PROTECT YOU!!

NOW, COME ON AND TAKE THE PILLS WITH ME!!
WE CAN HAVE OUR REVENGE TOGETHER!!
WE'LL KILL EVERY LAST ONE OF THEM!!
I...
I DON'T WANT TO.
STOP IT!!
DON (WHUMP)
GET AWAY FROM ME!!!
DA (DASH)
YOU TOO, HUH...
YOU'RE JUST LIKE YOUR MOTHER.

WHY DO YOU ALL REJECT POWER!!?
ZA (SLICE)
AAAAAAAAH!!
IF YOU DON'T WANT TO BE STOLEN FROM...
ZASHU (SLASH)
...YOU HAVE TO STEAL FROM OTHERS!!
ZASHU
WHY DOES NO ONE UNDER-STAND THAT!!!?
ZASHU
P-PLEASE...
IT HURTS...

HA HA!!! HAND OVER YOUR VALUABLES!!!
AH HA HA
HA
YOU'RE OBVIOUSLY A BANDIT, RIGHT!!?
THERIANTHROPE BANDITS ALWAYS FIGHT SO HARD! I LOVE IT!!!
HA
HA!

THE PAIN WAS SO HORRIBLE, I STARTED HEARING THINGS THAT WEREN'T THERE...
...AND WHEN I CAME TO, I WAS ALONE.
SOMEHOW, THE WOUNDS ON MY BACK HAD ALL CLOSED UP...
...AND SOMEHOW, ALL THE MEMBERS OF THE BIG CLAN THAT ATTACKED US WERE DEAD.
NO...
MOTHER ...

I LOST MY FRIENDS.
MY NEIGHBORS.
MY MOTHER.
AND MY BELOVED FIANCÉ HAD BECOME MY BITTER FOE.
I HAD NOTHING LEFT, SO I WAS FORCED TO SELL MY BODY TO GET BY.
I PUT EVERYTHING I HAD INTO PURSUING WEALTH AND POWER.
IF I DIDN'T WANT TO BE STOLEN FROM, I NEEDED TO STEAL FROM OTHERS.
IT WAS MY HATED NEMESIS WHO TAUGHT ME THAT, AND I INTENDED TO TAKE ALL HE POSSESSED.

...ULTI-MATELY, THE COMPANY AND THE MONEY MEAN NOTHING TO ME.
I DO APOLOGIZE FOR MAKING YOU TAKE PART IN MY QUEST FOR REVENGE.
UH-HUH...
CULTS, WEIRD AUDITORY HALLUCINATIONS... YEESH, I NEVER REALIZED THE WORLD WAS SUCH A SCARY PLACE.
AT LONG LAST...
...I WILL MAKE GETTAN PAY FOR WHAT HE DID!!

WAAAA (ROAR)
THINGS ARE STARTING TO GET UGLY.
RUMORS ABOUT THE COUNTERFEITS HAVE SPREAD, AND MORE PEOPLE ARE TRYING TO GET THEIR MONEY FROM THE MCA BY THE DAY.
THE CREDIT COLLAPSE IS BEGIN-NING.
I NEED TO HURRY UP AND TELL ALPHA...
TA (DASH)
...THAT WE DECODED MASTER SHADOW'S SECRET MESSAGE ...!!
end

THE Eminence IN Shadow

Episode.39

WHAT'S THIS WE'VE BEEN HEARING ABOUT COUNTER-FEITS!?
WHAT THE HELL HAVE YOU BEEN DOING WITH OUR MONEY!?
WE WERE IDIOTS FOR TRUSTING THESE SCRAPS OF PAPER.
WE WANT OUR GOLD BACK, AND WE WANT IT NOW!!!!
WAAAAA (ROAR)
...IT WOULD APPEAR THE MCA'S HIT THEIR LIMIT.
AAAA
LADY ALPHA ...
...WE'VE HAD AN UPTICK IN PEOPLE ASKING FOR THEIR GOLD BACK AT MITSUGOSHI BANK TOO.
IF ALL OUR DEPOSITORS COME RUSHING IN AT ONCE...
...WE WON'T HAVE ENOUGH GOLD ON HAND TO CASH THEM ALL OUT.

IT'S FINE.
THERE'S NO USE FIGHTING IT...
OUR LORD WAS THE ONE WHO CAUSED THE CREDIT COLLAPSE.
WE WERE WORTHLESS TO HIM, SO HE ABAN-DONED US.
THAT... THAT CAN'T BE WHAT'S HAPPEN-ING...!!
PACHI (CRACKLE)
PACHI
IT IS. HE GAVE US ALL THAT POWER AND KNOWLEDGE, AND LOOK HOW WE SQUAN-DERED IT.
I SWORE I WOULD DEVOTE MY LIFE TO THE SHADOW GARDEN.
IT WAS THE VERY FIRST PROMISE I EVER MADE HIM.
IF THIS IS WHAT HE WANTS...
...THEN I'M PREPARED TO FADE INTO OBLIVION.

W-WELL, I'M NOT!! WE CAN'T LET THINGS END LIKE THIS...!!
I APOLOGIZE FOR INTERRUPTING!
GACHA (CLICK)
GETTAN, THE MAN WE BELIEVE IS THE MCA'S DE FACTO LEADER...
KO (TP)
...IS AFFILIATED WITH THE CULT, JUST AS WE SUSPECTED.
HE WAS PLANNING ON TAKING DOWN MITSUGOSHI...
...BY USING COUNTERFEIT BILLS TO CAUSE A CREDIT COLLAPSE...
...BUT HE NEVER GOT A CHANCE TO PUT HIS PLAN INTO ACTION!
WELL, OF COURSE.
IT WASN'T THE CULT THAT MADE THE FAKE BILLS, IT WAS OUR LORD...
......?

HOLD ON.
GETTAN... AND BY EXTENSION THE MCA, HAS TIES TO THE CULT.
COULD IT BE THAT OUR LORD ALREADY KNEW?
BUT IF THAT'S THE CASE...
...THEN MAYBE THE ONES HE WAS REALLY TRYING TO CRUSH WERE—!?
LADY ALPHA!! I HAVE ANOTHER REPORT!!
TA (DASH)
HAA
HAA (PANT)
ETA OVER AT THE LAB...
...MANAGED TO DECODE MASTER SHADOW'S CIPHER!!

ONCE YOU READ IT...
...YOU'LL UNDERSTAND EXACTLY WHAT HE WAS DOING ...!!
SORRY, BUT I HAVE TO BETRAY YOU ALL.
A PARTNER AND I ARE PRINTING FAKE CASH AND CON-VERTING IT TO REAL MONEY.
KASA (RUSTLE)
WE'VE GATHERED UP ALL OUR GOLD AT THE FACILITY I ONCE VISITED WITH YOU TO RESCUE MY SISTER.
I KNOW YOU MIGHT RESENT ME FOR DOING THIS...
...BUT I BELIEVE IT WAS THE BEST OPTION AVAILABLE.
......!!
I GET IT.
SO, IN OTHER WORDS...

...HE SAW THROUGH THE CULT'S PLAN FASTER THAN ANY-ONE...
...AND USED IT AGAINST THEM...!!
NOW, HE'S TELLING US TO TAKE THE GOLD HE AMASSED BY CASHING IN HIS FAKE BILLS WITH THE MCA...
...AND USE IT TO WEATHER THE CREDIT COLLAPSE ...!!
WE COULDN'T OPERATE FREELY FOR FEAR OF EXPOSING THE LINK BETWEEN MITSUGOSHI AND THE SHADOW GARDEN.
THAT'S WHY HE HAD TO DO ALL OF THIS IN SECRET!!
HE HID HIS IDENTITY IN ORDER TO KEEP US AT ARM'S LENGTH UNTIL THE TIME WAS RIGHT.
KUSHA (CRUMPLE)
THEY SAY THAT IF YOU WANT TO FOOL THE ENEMY, YOU HAVE TO START BY FOOLING YOUR FRIENDS.

THANK GOODNESS.
BORO (SOB)
BORO
HE DIDN'T ABANDON US AFTER ALL!!
HE'S ALWAYS LOOKING AT THE BIGGER PICTURE.
THIS HERE WAS THE CONCLUSION HE SAW.
WHAT VISION IT MUST HAVE TAKEN...
OH, AND LADY ALPHA...
...I HAVE ONE MORE THING TO REPORT.

DELTA!!
PURU (QUIVER)
PURU
PURU
YOU'RE OKAY!!?
UM, UM, UM... PLEASE DON'T BE MAD AT ME.
I WAS ON ONE OF BOSS MAN'S CONFIDENTIAL SECRET MISSIONS...
MONYO (MUMBLE)
MONYO
IT'S FINE!! I UNDERSTAND.
HE GAVE YOU SOME SORT OF IMPORTANT TASK, DIDN'T HE?
...
GYU (SQUEEZE)
Y-YEAH!! I FOUND THE BLACK JUGGLER AND BEAT HIM UP REAL—
OOPS, THAT'S SUPPOSED TO BE CONFIDENTIAL AND SECRET!!
HE'S ALREADY GONE AND SET THE STAGE.
NOW, THE REST IS UP TO US.

ZA (ZSH)
LET'S GO RETRIEVE HIS GOLD...
...SO WE CAN GREET THE MASSES WITH OUR HEADS HELD HIGH!!
THE NEXT DAY...

IT'S GONE!!!!
WHERE'D ALL THE GOLD GO!!?
B-B-BUT HOW!!?
A-A-AND WHY!!?
GAKU (WOBBLE)
GAKU
GAKU
GAKU
DID YUKIME MOVE IT WITHOUT TELLING ME? OR DID IT GET STOLEN!?
GAKU
I DID MAKE THAT BIG SHOW OF GIVING BETA THAT CIPHER...
...BUT THERE'S NO WAY SHE COULD HAVE DECODED IT ALREADY!!!
※ SHE TOTALLY DID.
GAKU
WITHOUT THAT GOLD, I CAN'T SAVE MITSUGOSHI!!
I WAS GONNA WHISPER, "ALL ACCORDING TO PLAN... THE COLLAPSE HAS BEGUN..."
...WHILE POSING NEXT TO IT, BUT NOW THAT'S ALL RUINED!! ARRRRGH!!

MR. SMITH, WE HAVE A PROBLEM!!
WELL, WELL, WELL.
SU (SHFF)
IF IT ISN'T YUKIME'S AIDES, UH...
NATSU AND KANA, SIR!
YUKIME WENT MISSING AFTER SHE LEFT TO CONVERT THE CASH INTO GOLD!!
GETTAN MUST HAVE FOUND OUT ABOUT WHAT WE WERE DOING!!
HE DID!!?
I SEE.
GOOOOOO (RUMBLE)
SO, THIS WAS GETTAN'S DOING...!!
SUCH INTENSE MAGICAL FORCE ...!!
IS THIS... MR. SMITH'S RAGE!?

TELL ME WHERE THE BAS-TARD IS.
I'M GOING TO GO TAKE BACK WHAT'S MINE ...!!!
...I HEARD SOMEONE WITHDREW A MASSIVE AMOUNT OF GOLD RIGHT BEFORE THE CREDIT COLLAPSE BEGAN.
IT SOUNDED SUSPICIOUS, BUT WHEN I DECIDED TO LOOK INTO IT...

...I NEVER IMAGINED I WOULD FIND YOU BEHIND IT ALL...
...YUKIME!!
LONG HAVE I WAITED FOR THIS DAY.
GET-TAN.
THE MAJOR CORPORATE ALLIANCE IS DONE FOR.
ACCEPT THAT YOU'VE LOST.
HA.
THIS IS YOUR IDEA OF REVENGE!?
ALL I HAVE TO DO IS TAKE THAT GOLD BACK...
...AND I CAN STILL SALVAGE THE SITU-ATION!!!

ZAN (SLASH)
B...
GAKU (WOBBLE)
BUT HOW ...!!?
SINCE THAT DAY, I HAVE WORKED HARDER THAN YOU CAN IMAGINE.
NO LONGER AM I A LITTLE GIRL IN NEED OF PROTECTION.

(VWOO)
BEHOLD THE TRUE MIGHT OF THE SPIRIT FOX CLAN.
AS I AM NOW...
...YOU STAND NO CHANCE AGAINST ME.
W-WAIT, HOLD ON...
YUKIME...!!

PITA
(FREEZE)
...!?
HAAH...
SUU
(SHPP)
...I KNOW NOT WHAT IT WAS THAT CHANGED YOU SO.
BUT THE FACT REMAINS THAT YOU ONCE SAVED MY VILLAGE AND MY LIFE.
PEOPLE CANNOT ERASE THEIR GOOD DEEDS ANY MORE THAN THEY MAY THEIR SINS.

...I CHOOSE TO BELIEVE THAT THE MAN WHO SAVED ME...
...EXISTS WITHIN YOU STILL.
AND BECAUSE OF THAT...
THAT WAS ALL I WISHED TO TELL YOU.
FAREWELL, GETTAN...
FUU (HUFF)
FUU
RGH ...
ZARA (RATTLE)

DO (SHUNK)
THAT'S THE SAME NAÏVETÉ THAT GOT YOUR VILLAGE BURNED DOWN!!
HOW DO YOU STILL FAIL TO SEE THAT THE POWERLESS JUST GET TAKEN FROM!!!
ZUZU (SHLP)
AGH...
DOSA (SLUMP)
YOU WOULD REALLY TRY TO MAKE A MOCKERY OF ME LIKE THAT?
GETTAN, YOU DIDN'T...
YOU TOOK THE PILLS...!!?

PITA (FREEZE)
...AND THERE HE IS.
I'D FIGURED I'D BE SEEING YOU...
...JOHN SMITH.

YOU STOLE WHAT I HOLD MOST DEAR ...!!!
IT WAS YOU.
HA! WHAT, YOU MEAN THIS WOMAN?
WELL, TOO BAD.
BECAUSE YOU WON'T BE TAKING BACK A THING!!!
DA (DASH)
I DIS-AGREE.
HYURU (SHWP)
I THINK YOU'LL FIND I HAVE A WAY OF GETTING WHAT I WANT.

NII (GRIN)
SUU (FWAA)
ZAN (SLASH)

DODGED IT, DID YOU?
EVER SINCE I LOST MY VISION...
...MY ABILITY TO DETECT MAGIC HAS ADVANCED BY LEAPS AND BOUNDS.
I HATE TO BREAK IT TO YOU, BUT I CAN SENSE EVERY MOVE YOUR THREADS MAKE.
YOUR THREADS MIGHT BE DIFFICULT TO SEE...
...BUT I KNOW EXACTLY WHERE ALL OF THEM ARE!!!
...IS THAT SO.
IN THAT CASE...
...WHY NOT COME OVER HERE AND SAY THAT TO MY FACE?

...!!
ZOKU (SHUDDER)
DON'T FALL FOR HIS BAIT.
THE FACT I CAN SENSE THEIR POSITION...
...MEANS I KNOW JUST HOW DEVIOUSLY HE'S DEPLOYED THEM!!
IF I GO IN THERE WITHOUT A PLAN, HE'LL SLICE ME TO RIBBONS!!
BUT THAT'S NOT THE WORST PART.
WHAT I WANT TO KNOW IS...
...WHAT'S UP WITH THAT OVERPOWERING AURA OF RAGE HE'S GIVING OFF!!!?

COULD THAT BE A SIGN...
...OF JUST HOW MUCH HE CARES ABOUT YUKIME!!?
OUT WITH IT.
I THINK YOU HAVE SOMETHING TO SAY TO ME.
...
WE'RE PAST THE POINT OF WORDS.
THERE'S NO TURNING BACK FOR ME.
I'VE ALREADY SACRI-FICED TOO MUCH...
ZARA (RATTLE)
...IN THE PURSUIT OF POWER!!!

I HAVE TO STEAL BEFORE I'M STOLEN FROM!!!
EVEN IF THAT MEANS ...
GOO (RRRMB)
...LAYING DOWN MY OWN LIFE!!!
WITH MY NEW STRENGTH ...
...YOUR STEEL WIRES ARE LIKE TISSUE PAPER TO ME!!!!
...YOU HAVE A POINT.
STEEL IS FLIMSY.
SU (SHFF)

GO (SMACK)
WHA...
GAH!!
IF MIGHT MAKES RIGHT...
ZA (ZSH)
...THEN MAKE RIGHT WITH MIGHT.

BOKI (CRACK)
DOGA (BIFF)
BAKI (SNAP)
MERI (RIP)
GAGI (KLUDD)
MISHI (CRUNCH)
GOKI (THOK)
BEKI (FWAP)
BAKI
DA (DASH)

GOKI
(THOK)
MISHI
(CRUNCH)
BAKI
(SNAP)
MISHI
GOKI
BEKI
(F-WAP)
GOKI
SHI

OOO (VWOO)
DOGOO (KAWHAM)
BA (WSHH)
YORO (STAGGER)
HAA... HAA...
HIT ME ALL YOU LIKE!!
THANKS TO THE PILLS, MY WOUNDS HEAL INSTANTLY!!!

GAGI (KLUDD)
GOGA (POW)
GOGI (THWAK)
GI
BEGI (FWLINK)

BAKI (SNAP)
DOGO (WHAM)
DOKA (WHUMP)
BAKI

SAY IT.
GAHA (HACK)
GOHO (KOFF)
YOU KNOW WHAT I WANT TO HEAR!!!
NO MATTER WHAT I SAY NOW ...
...IT'S ALREADY TOO LATE!!!

GO
(SMASH)
......!!
SO THAT'S WHAT THIS IS.
I KNOW THIS ATTACK.
JOHN SMITH ...
...YOU'RE THE MAN FROM BACK THEN...

AH...
I WONDER...
...IF I HAD POWER LIKE YOURS...
...WOULD MY LIFE HAVE PLAYED OUT DIFFERENTLY?
end

THE Eminence IN Shadow

Episode.40
HAA...
HAA...
HAA...
SHIN (STILL)

THE PILLS WORE OFF...
HAA...
THIS IS AS FAR AS I GO...
HAA...
HURGH !!?
DO (WHAM)
COME ON.
OUT WITH IT.
......
TELL ME WHERE YOU HID THE GOLD YOU STOLE!!!
HE WANTS ME TO APOLOGIZE BEFORE I DIE...TO TELL HER I'M SORRY...

...I MADE...
...SOME BAD CALLS.
GEHO (GACK)
GOHO (KOFF)
ALL THIS TIME...I'VE BEEN FLEEING FROM MY OWN WEAKNESS.
I WAS SO AFRAID OF LOSING THINGS, I THREW EVERYTHING I HAD INTO PURSUING STRENGTH...
BEFORE I KNEW IT, I'D LOST SIGHT OF WHAT IT WAS I WAS TRYING TO PROTECT.
I WAS LOST...
...ADRIFT IN A LIGHTLESS VOID...
KOFF!
HAKK...
I RESPECT... YOUR DEVOTION.
SO I'LL TELL YOU... ABOUT WHAT...
SU (POINT)
...I TRULY... WANTED TO PROTECT...

I EN-
TRUST...
...YOU...
...WITH...
...YU...

YOU GOT IT.
I READ YOU...
...LOUD AND CLEAR!!
GASHI (GRAB)
THANK...
...GOODNESS...

SURU (SMOOTH)
WE'RE SO GLAD YOU'RE ALL RIGHT, MA'AM.
EVEN THE SCARS ON YOUR BACK ARE GONE!
IT WAS MR. JOHN WHO HEALED ME.
WHEN I FELT HIS MAGIC, IT MADE ME REALIZE...
...THAT THIS WAS THE SECOND TIME HE HAS SAVED ME.

THERE IS SUCH A WARMTH TO HIS STRENGTH.
MY HEART FROZE OVER ALL THOSE YEARS AGO...
...BUT NOW, HE HAS FINALLY THAWED IT...
KO (TMP)
KO
GI (CREAK)
WHAT...? THE VAULT...
...IS EMPTY!?
JUDGING BY YOUR REACTION...
...I TAKE IT HE HASN'T FILLED YOU IN YET.
!!?

WE'VE ALREADY RETRIEVED ...
...ALL THE GOLD THAT WAS IN THE VAULT.
I AM ALPHA, FROM THE SHADOW GARDEN.
KO (TMP)
AND YOU'RE YUKIME OF THE SNOW FOX CORPORATION.
PARTNER TO OUR MUTUAL FRIEND...
...AND THE WOMAN THAT GETTAN OF THE MCA WAS FIXATED ON.
I CAME TO DELIVER THIS LETTER TO YOU.
I DID HAVE TO READ IT AS PART OF OUR INVESTIGATION...
...BUT WE FOUND IT IN GETTAN'S ROOM ADDRESSED TO YOU.

...PERHAPS IT WAS LESS A LETTER AND MORE OF A LAST WILL.
IT MUST HAVE BEEN DIFFICULT TO WRITE WITH HIS LOST SIGHT...
...AS THE HANDWRITING IS BY NO MEANS NEAT.
IN IT, HE EXPRESSES HOW SORRY HE IS FOR WHAT HE DID TO YOU AND YOUR HOME-TOWN...
...AND DESCRIBES THE CULT OF DIABLOS...
...THE ORGANIZATION THAT GUIDED HIS ACTIONS.
THE CULT OF DIABLOS ...!
GIRI (GRIND)
WE OF THE SHADOW GARDEN STAND AGAINST THEM.
AND SO DOES LORD SHADOW... OR AS YOU KNEW HIM, JOHN SMITH.
EVERYTHING HE DID, HE DID IN PURSUIT OF THAT GOAL.
SU (SHFF)

BECAUSE MITSU-GOSHI...
SARA (SWAY)
...IS SECRETLY A FRONT FOR THE SHADOW GARDEN.
HE DIDN'T JOIN YOUR SCHEME IN ORDER TO GET RICH.
HE DID IT SO MITSUGOSHI WOULD HAVE THE CAPITAL TO SURVIVE THE CREDIT COLLAPSE.
......!!
EVERYTHING PLAYED OUT EXACTLY ACCORDING TO HIS DESIGNS.
THE MCA'S FALL WILL ALLOW US TO CAPTURE THEIR MARKET SHARE...
...AND ESTABLISH AN UNAS-SAILABLE POSITION.
NOT EVEN MIDGAR WILL BE ABLE TO LAY A FINGER ON US.
IF MITSUGOSHI CEASED OPERATIONS, THE KINGDOM'S ECONOMY WOULD CRUMBLE.

...AND MR. SHADOW INTENDS TO USE THAT NEWFOUND POWER...
...TO CORNER AND CHECKMATE THE CULT?
EXACT-LY.
AND TO THAT END, IF YOU'RE INTERESTED...
...WE WOULD LIKE FOR THE SNOW FOX CORPORATION TO ACT AS OUR LIAISON WITHIN THE LAWLESS CITY.
YOU'RE PROBABLY FEELING RATHER BETRAYED RIGHT NOW...
...BUT I'M SURE LORD SHADOW IS FULLY PREPARED TO ACCEPT YOUR RESENTMENT.
......

PERISH THE THOUGHT.
HE HAS SAVED ME NOW TWICE OVER.
I FEEL NOTHING TOWARD HIM BUT GRATITUDE.
FROM HERE ON, MITSUGOSHI SHALL CONTINUE ACTING AS THE PUBLIC FACE...
GU (SHAKE)
...WHILE THE SNOW FOX CORPORATION WILL HANDLE THE DIRTY WORK...A CLEVER ARRANGEMENT.
I'M GLAD WE COULD SEE EYE TO EYE ON THIS.
WE'LL BE IN TOUCH...
ZAAAA (WHOOSH)
...MS. YUKIME.

ZAAA
I MUST SAY, IT IS QUITE A SHAME...
...THAT HE ALREADY HAS SO MANY PEOPLE PRECIOUS TO HIM.
PERHAPS I SHOULD NOT BE SUR-PRISED.
HE EVEN WENT SO FAR AS TO STAY BEHIND...
...SAYING HE HAD ONE LAST JOB TO DO—DIGGING GETTAN A GRAVE.
NEVER IN ALL MY DAYS...
...HAVE I MET A MAN WITH SO BROAD A HEART...
ZA (SHUNK)

AFTER THAT, I SPENT AGES DIGGING.
WE HATED EACH OTHER, WE FOUGHT TO THE DEATH, AND IN THE END, WE DEVELOPED A MUTUAL RESPECT.
THAT'S WHY I'M DIGGING HOLES BASED ON HIS FINAL WORDS.
THE LAST WORD HE SAID TO ME WAS "YEW"...
...AND HE POINTED THIS WAY.
IN OTHER WORDS, HE BURIED THE STOLEN GOLD NEAR THE YEW TREES OVER HERE.
I STILL CAN'T SEEM TO FIND IT, THOUGH. DUNNO WHY.

I ALSO DON'T KNOW...
...WHY YUKIME AND THE GIRLS HAVEN'T COME TO SHOUT AT ME YET.
YOU TOOK THINGS TOO FAR THIS TIME.
WHERE'S MY MONEY, MISTER?
FROM WHAT I HEAR, IT BARELY TOOK ANY TIME AT ALL FOR THE MCA TO CRUMBLE.
PEOPLE WERE GETTING WORRIED, SO IN ORDER TO CALM THINGS DOWN...
...THE KNIGHT ORDER GOT INVOLVED AND FORCED THE MCA TO OPEN THEIR VAULT.
PROBLEM WAS, THERE WAS WAY LESS GOLD THAN PAPER BILLS IN CIRCULA-TION.
THAT MADE PEOPLE PANIC...
...AND MITSUGOSHI BANK WAS THEIR NEXT STOP.

BUT WHEN THEY GOT THERE, THEY FOUND MOUNTAINS OF GOLD PILED UP...
...AND TELLERS WEARING CALM, CONFIDENT SMILES AS THEY EXCHANGED MONEY.
SEEING THAT RENEWED PUBLIC TRUST IN MITSU-GOSHI...
...AND EVENTU-ALLY, THE WHOLE THING DIED DOWN.
I DON'T HAVE A CLUE WHEN THE GIRLS FOUND THE TIME TO STASH AWAY ALL THAT MONEY...
...BUT THERE IS ONE THING I KNOW FOR SURE.
PHEW...

MY BIG "EVERYTHING I DID, I DID TO SAVE MITSUGOSHI!!" PLAN...
...IS COMPLETELY RUINED.
Y'KNOW, THIS IS KIND OF A PAIN. WHAT IF I JUST BLASTED A MASSIVE HOLE IN THE GROUND?
OH WAIT, THAT'D VAPORIZE THE BURIED GOLD TOO...
AND AS FOR THE STRAY DOG WHO TRACKED ME HERE BY SCENT...
I CAN'T FIND ANYTHING, BOSS MAN!!
BA (WSHH)
BA
BA
IS THIS ANOTHER CONFIDENTIAL SECRET MISSION!!?
YUP.
SO YOU CAN'T GO TELLING ALPHA OR THE OTHERS ABOUT IT.
BA
BA
BA

BA
BA
BA (WSHH)
AND WHEN WE'RE DONE HERE, YOU'LL DO WHATEVER I SAY, RIGHT!?
WHAT'RE YOU TALKING ABOUT?
YOU PROMISED, BOSS MAN!!
I'M PRETTY SURE THAT'S NOT EXACTLY WHAT I AGREED TO...
BA
BA
BA
BA
BA
BUT YOU SAID YOU'D GIVE ME WHATEVER I ASKED FOR...!!!
PURU
PURU
PURU (QUIVER)
LOOK, THERE ARE SOME WISHES I CAN'T GRANT. I'M NOT SANTA, AFTER ALL.
WHO'S SANTA?
A GUY WHO SAYS HE'LL MAKE ANY WISH COME TRUE...
...BUT IS SECRETLY A MONSTROUS DEVIL DRESSED IN CRIMSON WHO REFUSED TO GRANT MY HEART'S DESIRE.
OH, I GOT IT... HERE'S WHAT WE'LL DO.

I'M ABOUT TO GO ON A JOURNEY.
WHY DON'T YOU SPEND THE TIME I'M GONE THINKING ABOUT WHAT YOU WANT?
A JOURNEY!?
THE GIRLS ARE PROBABLY TOTALLY PISSED AT ME.
I HAVE A BAD FEELING ABOUT WHAT WOULD HAPPEN IF I RAN INTO THEM.
AFTER ALL THE SHIT I PULLED...
ANGER IS AN EMOTION THAT DWINDLES WITH TIME, SO I GOTTA LET THEM COOL OFF.
MY ACADEMY'S ON WINTER BREAK, SO THE TIMING IS PERFECT.
ALL I HAVE TO DO IS COME BACK WHEN BREAK IS OVER AND PLAY DUMB LIKE NOTHING HAPPENED.
THAT'S THE ULTIMATE HIDDEN NORMIE TECHNIQUE—
THE "UGH, THERE'S NO POINT TRYING TO REASON WITH THIS GUY" STANCE!!!

AND HEY.
MITSUGOSHI ENDED UP SURVIVING, SO THEY'LL PROBABLY FORGIVE ME SOMEDAY.
OOH, I COULD PAY THE ORIANA KINGDOM A VISIT!
I WONDER IF PRESIDENT ROSE EVER BECAME QUEEN.
WASHI (MUSS)
THANKS FOR HELPING OUT, DELTA.
WASHI
YOU CAN STOP DIGGING NOW.
SEE YA LATER!!
DOU (VOOM)
BOSS MAN, WAIT ...!!
THERE'S SOMETHING IN THE GROUND WHERE WE WERE JUST DIGGING—
OH... HE'S GONE.

AFTER TRYHARD DASHING OFF ON MY JOURNEY SO I WOULDN'T HAVE TO GRANT DELTA'S WISH...
...I REMINISCED ABOUT HOW THE FIRST TIME SANTA BETRAYED ME...
...WAS ON A SNOWY NIGHT MUCH LIKE THIS ONE.
...I OWE HIM MY THANKS.
I REALLY DO.

HIS METHODS CAN BE HEAVY-HANDED AT TIMES...
...BUT HE ALWAYS MAKES SURE WE WALK AWAY SMILING.
IT'S ALMOST AS THOUGH...
...HE'S A DEVIL DRESSED IN BLACK WHO WILL MAKE ANY WISH COME TRUE.

...DESPICABLE.
WHAT YOU DID WAS DESPICABLE, ROSE.
AND I WILL NEVER, EVER...
...FORGIVE YOU.

I'M SORRY!
I'M SOR—
HAA... HAA...
THAT SAME DREAM AGAIN...
DON
DON (BANG)
WHAT ARE YOU LAZING ABOUT FOR, 666?
YOU'RE LATE!
I...I'LL BE RIGHT OUT!!

ON THAT DAY...
...I KILLED MY FATHER, WHO HAD BEEN TURNED INTO PERV'S PUPPET, WITH MY OWN HANDS.
AFTER BECOMING A WANTED WOMAN, I DRIFTED OVER TO THE SHADOW GARDEN.
NOBODY HERE DIGS INTO ONE ANOTHER'S PASTS.
BUT IN RETURN, WE HAVE TO GIVE UP OUR NAMES AND OUR STATUSES.
SURURU (SHLUP)
NOW, I'M JUST NEW RECRUIT NUMBER 666.

THESE SLIME BODYSUITS CAME AS QUITE THE SHOCK AT FIRST.
THEY CONDUCT MAGIC SO WELL, AND THEY'RE QUITE STURDY.
I WAS AMAZED AT HOW GROUND-BREAKING THEY WERE.
IN FACT, THE SHADOW GARDEN BASES ARE FULL OF ALL SORTS OF NOVEL TECH-NOLOGY.
JUST WHO IS THE FANCY BANDIT SLAYER...
...OR RATHER, SHADOW, THE MAN WHOSE SHADOW WISDOM INSPIRED IT ALL?
MORNING, 666.
NUMBER 559 CALLED FOR US.
LET'S GET A MOVE ON. I'M THE ONE WHO'LL GET BLAMED IF WE'RE LATE!!

ALSO, I HEARD YOU JUST NOW.
THE SCREAMING.
I CAN TELL YOU CAME HERE UNDER UNIQUE CIRCUM-STANCES.
IF YOU'RE HAVING A ROUGH TIME, DON'T FORGET YOU CAN COME TALK TO ME!
I'M FINE.
...OH, NO.
IF YOU SAY SO.
I THOUGHT JOINING THE SHADOW GARDEN WOULD LET ME MAKE A DIFFER-ENCE...
...BUT I HAVEN'T ACCOM-PLISHED ANYTHING YET.
OH, CID...
...DID I MAKE THE RIGHT CHOICE?

ZAA (WHOOSH)
THERE YOU ARE.
YOU'RE LATE.
I APOLOGIZE FOR OUR TARDINESS...
... NUMBER 559.
I'M GOING TO CUT RIGHT TO THE CHASE.
YOU SEE THE FORT OVER THERE?

THE ORIANA KINGDOM HAS BEEN DIVIDED INTO PERV AND ANTI-PERV FACTIONS, AND SMALL SKIRMISHES HAVE BEEN BREAKING OUT HERE AND THERE.
TWO DAYS AGO, FORT FIRST FELL INTO THE PERV FACTION'S HANDS.
IT'S A SMALL FORTRESS THAT SITS ON THE ORIANA-MIDGAR BORDER, AND IT HOLDS LITTLE STRATEGIC SIGNIFICANCE.
YET IN SPITE OF THAT, THE CULT IS DEPLOYING THEIR FINEST TROOPS THERE—
THE FIRST CHILDREN.
THEY'RE UP TO SOMETHING, THAT MUCH IS CERTAIN.
OUR MISSION IS TO INFILTRATE THE FORT AND IDENTIFY THE CULT'S OBJECTIVE.

DO YOU KNOW WHY YOU WERE SELECTED FOR THIS TASK...
...ROSE ORIANA?
!!?
OH, UM ...
IS IT... BECAUSE OF HOW FAMILIAR I AM WITH THE AREA?
THE ROYAL FAMILY SOMETIMES USED THAT FORT AS A SUMMER HOME.
PRECISELY.
BUT THAT ISN'T ALL.
I ASKED FOR YOU PERSONALLY.

MASTER SHADOW GRANTED YOU POWER, DIDN'T HE?
HE DID...!?
ZAWA (MURMUR)
OOH, LUCKY YOU.
THE ONLY ONES MASTER SHADOW PERSONALLY EMPOWERED WERE THE INITIAL SEVEN—
THE SEVEN SHADOWS.
I ASSUME YOU'RE AWARE THAT THEY POSSESS ABILITIES BEYOND THAT OF THE REST OF THE SHADOW GARDEN.
ASIDE FROM THEM, THE ONLY PEOPLE WHO'VE RECEIVED THAT SPECIAL POWER ARE YOU...
...AND ME.
HOWEVER, I FIND IT HARD TO IMAGINE YOU BEING STRONG ENOUGH TO DESERVE IT.

IF YOU PROVE TO BE AN IMPEDIMENT ON THIS MISSION...
...I'LL DISCARD YOU ON THE SPOT.
GOKU (GULP)
I AM MASTER SHADOW'S FAITHFUL SERVANT.
AND I SHALL PURGE ANY WHO ARE UNWORTHY OF HIM...
...WITHOUT A SHRED OF MERCY OR REMORSE.
end

Episode.41

FORT FIRST
CASTLE TOWN
OH, WOW.
YOU CAME ALL THE WAY FROM MIDGAR?
YOU KNOW, I USED TO TURN TRICKS OVER IN THE LAWLESS CITY.
I DID VISIT THE ROYAL CAPITAL A FEW TIMES WHEN I LIVED IN THE AREA.
IT'S SUCH A LOVELY CITY.
KARAN (CLINK)
I DUNNO ABOUT THAT.
I THINK THE LAWLESS CITY'S PRETTY SWEET, MYSELF.

I THINK OF IT AS A SORT OF HOME AWAY FROM HOME.
KARARA (CLINK)
I HEAR IT'S BEEN PRETTY CHAOTIC THERE LATELY, THOUGH.
IT REALLY HAS... WHEN THE RED MOON APPEARED, IT GOT OVERRUN WITH GHOULS.
THE BROTHEL I WORKED AT GOT COMPLETELY TRASHED.
BUT THEN, A MAN SHOWED UP AND SAVED ME...
I WANT A CHANCE TO THANK HIM SOMEDAY.
THAT'S WHY I OPENED THIS TAVERN.

I KEEP THINKING HOW NICE IT WOULD BE IF HE JUST HAPPENED TO STROLL THROUGH THAT DOOR SOMEDAY.
...BUT I GUESS THAT'S HOPING FOR TOO MUCH.
NAH, THAT'S A GREAT STORY. I DUNNO WHO THAT GUY WAS, BUT I'M ROOTING FOR YOU.
THE PROBLEM IS...THINGS AREN'T ALL SUNSHINE AND RAINBOWS HERE IN ORIANA EITHER.
HEH HEH.
JUST THE OTHER DAY, PERV'S MEN TOOK OVER THE TOWN, AND—
BAN (SLAM)
HEY, MARIE!!
WE'RE HERE TO TAKE YOUR EARNINGS FOR THE DAY!!
YOU'RE BEHIND ON YOUR PAYMENTS, SO MAKE IT SNAPPY!!!

BUT I PAID YOU JUST THE OTHER DAY...!!
Y-YOU SOLDIERS ARE BACK ALREADY!?
GATA (TREMBLE)
RENT'S GONE UP. THAT LAST PAYMENT WON'T CUT IT!!
IF YOU DON'T HAVE THE MONEY, WE'LL STRING YOU UP FOR TREASON!!
HYAH HA HA HA HA!
BUT THAT'S NOT FAIR!!
WOW, THOSE SOLDIERS ARE A BUNCH OF ASSHOLES.
AND RIGHT WHEN I WAS ENJOYING THIS GLASS OF APPLE JUICE IN TRUE HARD-BOILED FASHION TOO.
SORO (SNEAK)
SORO
SHOULD I MAKE A BREAK FOR IT LIKE THE REST OF THE NOBODIES ...?
NAH, SCREW THAT.
I'M ON VACATION.
GARA (CLATTER)

C-CUT IT OUT!!
DAN (STOMP)
IT'S TIME TO LET LOOSE A BIT!!
AND SO, A BRAVE YOUNG BOY...
...STANDS UP TO THE PAIR OF TYRANNICAL SOLDIERS.
ZA (ZSH)
THAT'S RIGHT —
IT'S MY TIME TO SHINE!!!
KATA
KATA
KATA (TREMBLE)
LEAVE MARIE ALONE!!
DEAR CUSTOMER, NO!!
HA-HA. SOUNDS LIKE YOU WANT A PIECE OF ME, KID!!
WELL, HEY!
BA (WSHH)
THAT'S FINE BY ME!!

MY LOVE IS INVINCI-BLE!!!
KA (KSHHH)
BEHOLD, MY HARD-BOILED NORMIE TECHNIQUE!!
WHERE A BOY FINDS HIS HIDDEN STRENGTH THROUGH THE POWER OF LOVE...

...AND PUNCHES THE BADDIES INTO NEXT WEEK!!!

PAKYA (SMASH)
OH, SHADDAP.
MARIE... I'M GLAD I GOT TO SPEND MY FINAL MOMENTS CALLING OUT YOUR NAME...
THAT WAS PERFECT... IT'S NOT A REAL BAR FIGHT UNTIL SOMEONE GETS A BOTTLE SMASHED OVER THEIR HEAD.
...OR SO HE THINKS, BUT AS SOON AS HE GETS COCKY, THEY MOP THE FLOOR WITH HIM!!
BATAAN (THUD)
DEAR CUS-TOM-ER!!
HA-HA-HA!! THIS IS WHAT HAP-PENS WHEN YOU TRY TO DEFY US, DUMBASS!!

THE MONEY IS BEHIND THE COUNTER.
JUST TAKE IT AND LEAVE!!
HEH. SHOULDA JUST TOLD US THAT FROM THE START!!
URGH... I'M SORRY I MESSED THAT UP...
PURU (QUIVER)
PURU
IT DOESN'T MATTER. WHAT'S IMPORTANT IS GETTING YOU PATCHED UP!!
I'M USED TO VIOLENCE, SO I'LL BE FINE.
I SHOULD HAVE KNOWN...
...THAT MY MYSTERY MAN WOULDN'T BE COMING TO SAVE ME TODAY...

JARA (JANGLE)
HEH-HEH. LIKE TAKIN' CANDY FROM A BABY.
JARA
YOU SURE IT'S OKAY FOR US TO BE RIPPING OFF THE LOCALS LIKE THIS?
IT'S FINE! IT'S NOT LIKE ANYONE'S GONNA FIND OUT.
HA HA
HA HA!
WITH THE KING DEAD AND THE PRINCESS MISSING...
...PERV ASSHAT BASICALLY CONTROLS THE ENTIRE KINGDOM.
IT'S NOT LIKE HE'S GONNA PUNISH HIS OWN SOLDIERS FOR GETTING INTO A LITTLE MISCHIEF.
AND BESIDES...
NII (GRIN)
...I HEAR THAT WE'RE GONNA BE ORDERED TO WIPE OUT THE WHOLE TOWN BEFORE LONG ANYWAYS.

THOSE CULT GUYS DON'T MESS AROUND.
THE TOWN'S CLOSE TO SOME IMPORTANT RUIN OR SOME-THING...
...SO THEY WANT TO MAKE SURE NO ONE BLABS ABOUT—
KOTSU (STEP)
WHO'S THERE?
THE KID FROM EARLIER!?
ARE... ARE YOU HERE FOR PAYBACK OR SOME-THING!?
IN THAT CASE, YOU CAN BE THE FIRST TO DIE!!
BA (WSHH)

OOH, GOING STRAIGHT FOR THE KILL?
I LOVE IT.
REMINDS ME OF THE LAWLESS CITY, MY HOME AWAY FROM HOME.
I PICKED A LOT OF POCKETS BACK THERE.
SU (SHLUCK)
......!!
GOBA (HURK)

BUT YOU GUYS SEEM KINDA BROKE...
...SO I GUESS I'LL HAVE TO SETTLE FOR STEALING THESE.
EEK!! YOU RIPPED OUT HIS HEART WITH YOUR BARE HANDS!?
WHAT KIND OF MONSTER ARE YOU...?
DOSA (SLUMP)
IT'S LIKE YOU'RE A WHOLE DIFFERENT PERSON THAN—
DO (DOOF)
IN MY HOME AWAY FROM HOME, MIGHT MAKES RIGHT.
AND I'VE GOT THE MIGHT...
ZURU (SHLUP)

...SO I'M ALWAYS RIGHT.
GUSHA (SPLURT)
※ THIS IS OUR PROTAGONIST.
WHEW.
HEARTS ARE LIKE BATTERIES. WHEN THEY GO BAD, YOU GOTTA POP 'EM OUT.
BOTA
BOTA (DRIP)
THAT STUFF THEY WERE SAYING ABOUT A RUIN SOUNDED KINDA INTERESTING.
I GOTTA STOP BACK BY THE TAVERN TO PAY FOR MY APPLE JUICE...
...BUT THEN, IT'S SIGHT-SEEING TIME!!

DOSHA (WHUMP)
WHAT WAS THAT SOUND!?
THOSE SOLDIERS DIDN'T COME BACK, DID THEY!?
BIKU (TWITCH)
BASA (FLUTTER)
BAN (BAM)
WAIT... WHAT!?
IT'S THE TAVERN EARNINGS THEY MADE OFF WITH!!
......
I DON'T BELIEVE IT.
COULD THAT REALLY HAVE BEEN HIM...!?

NEXT TIME, YOU SHOULD COME ON IN.
I'LL SAVE A SPECIAL DRINK JUST FOR YOU...
WHEN WE FOLLOWED THOSE SHADY CULT MEMBERS WHO SNUCK OUT OF THE FORT...
...I NEVER EXPECTED TO FIND A RUIN ALL THE WAY OUT HERE.

THAT USED TO BE A TEMPLE HONORING THE WARRIORS WHO PERISHED IN THE FIGHT AGAINST THE DEMON DIABLOS.
IT FELL INTO DISREPAIR, SO IT SHOULD BE EMPTY...
...BUT THEY WOULD NEVER BRING SO MANY FIRST CHILDREN UNLESS THERE WAS SOMETHING IMPORTANT THERE.
ALSO, I RECOGNIZE THAT MAN...HE'S KOUADOI THE GALE.
ONE OF THE CULT'S LEADERS ...!!
AND NEXT TO HIM...
!?
NO.
IT CAN'T BE...!!

MOTHER!!?
WHAT'S MY MOTHER DOING HERE!?
I THOUGHT SHE WAS BEING KEPT SAFE SOMEWHERE BEYOND PERV'S CLUTCHES!!
KEEP IT DOWN!
THEY'RE DOING SOMETHING!!
NOW, PLACE YOUR HAND UPON THE ALTAR...
...QUEEN REINA.
SU (SHFF)

PAA (SHINE)
ZUA (VWOOM)
AAA (WHOOSH)
IS THAT... A RING?
...PREPARE FOR BATTLE.
ZA (ZSH)
WE'RE RETRIEV- ING THAT RING!!
WHAT!?
BUT MY MOTHER'S DOWN THERE ...!!

THAT'S NONE OF OUR CON-CERN.
THAT RING IS LIKELY THE KEY.
WE NEED TO TAKE IT FROM THEM, NO MATTER THE COST!!
BA (WSHH)
H-HOLD ON!! THEY HAVE US HUGELY OUTNUM-BERED...!!
TA
TA (DASH)
TA
TA
TA

ZASHU (SLASH)
!!
THEY'RE HERE!!
IT'S THE SHADOW GARDEN !!
ZAN (SHLUPP)
HURGH!!

AH...
EEK...
ZASHU (SLASH)
ZASHU
GIRO (GLARE)
AAAH ...!!
BA (WSHH)

ZUSHAA (SHWIP)
ARE YOU ALL RIGHT, MOTHER!?
BA (WSHH)
R... ROSE!?
WHAT ARE YOU DOING HERE...!?
HEY!!
DO YOU PLAN ON GETTING IN MY WAY, NUMBER 666!!?
O-OF COURSE I DO!!
WHY DID YOU ATTACK MY MOTHER JUST NOW!?
YOU NEED TO EXPLAIN WHAT OUR MISSION IS ACTUALLY TRYING TO—
SU (SHFF)

ZA (ZSH)
NOBODY MOVE.
TRY ANY FUNNY BUSINESS, AND THE TWO OF THEM GET IT.
SURPRISE ATTACK OR NOT...
...THE FACT REMAINS YOU TOOK OUT NINE OF OUR FIRST CHILDREN.
IS THIS THE POWER OF THE FABLED SEVEN SHADOWS?
I HATE TO BREAK IT TO YOU, BUT I DON'T NUMBER AMONG THEIR RANKS.
NOT YET, AT LEAST.
OH? YOU'RE JUST A FOOT SOLDIER?
THAT MAKES IT ALL THE MORE IMPRESSIVE, THEN.

BUT NOW, WE HAVE HOSTAGES.
EEK!!
THEY HAVE THE UPPER HAND HERE. WE NEED TO PULL OUT—
NUMBER 559!!
...DO WHAT YOU LIKE WITH THE HOSTAGES.
THAT WRETCH INTERFERED WITH MY MISSION!!
THAT MAKES HER A TRAITOR TO THE SHADOW GARDEN.
BA (WSHH)
I'LL GET RID OF YOU ALL IN ONE FELL SWOOP!!!
I HAD NO IDEA THE SHADOW GARDEN'S METHODS WERE SO BARBARIC!!
HMPH.
YOU CAN'T—

PRINCESS ROSE SHOWING UP WAS THE BEST THING WE COULD HAVE ASKED FOR.
GET THE TWO OF THEM TO PERV ON THE DOUBLE!!
AS YOU WISH.
NUMBER 664, WHAT SHOULD WE DOOO?
THE ONLY THING WE CAN DO NOW...
WE'LL JUST HAVE ...
...TO FIGHT OUR WAY OUT OF HERE!!!
WAA (SHOUT)

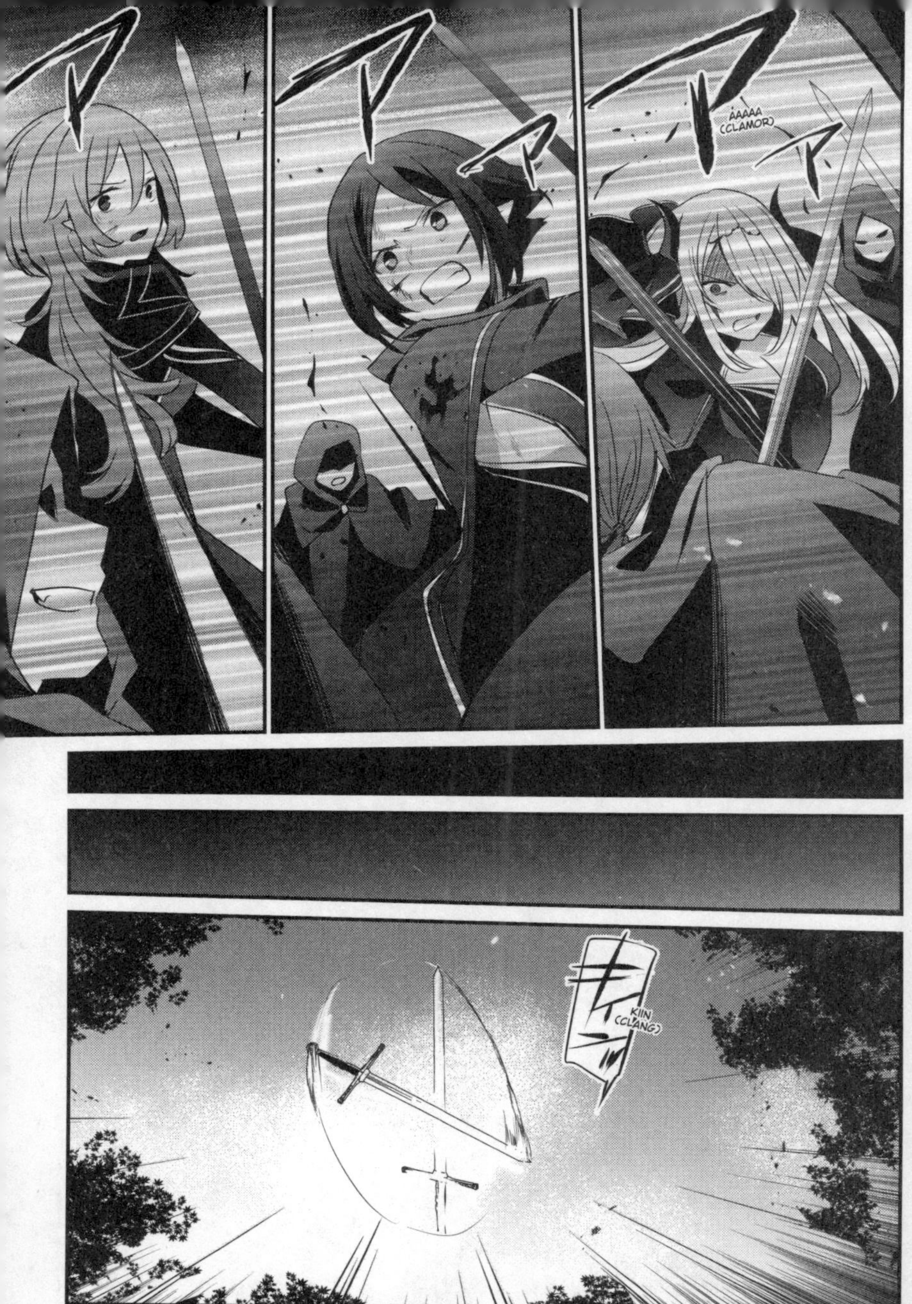
AAAAA
(CLAMOR)
KIIN
(CLANG)

POTA (DRIP)
POTA
...I HAVE TO SAY, I'M SHOCKED.
FURA (TOTTER)
I CAN'T BELIEVE YOU SURVIVED THIS LONG AGAINST THAT MANY FIRST CHILDREN...
...AND A MEMBER OF THE CULT'S LEADERSHIP.

TO BE HONEST, I WOULD WANT TO COMPLIMENT YOU...
...IF YOU WEREN'T SO OBVIOUSLY ON YOUR LAST LEGS!!!
DO (WHAM)
GAKH !!
I CAN TELL YOU DON'T HAVE ENOUGH MAGIC LEFT TO HEAL YOUR WOUNDS...
...BUT I'M NOT LETTING YOU DIE THAT EASY.
DOSA (FWUMP)

HOW DARE YOU ROB US OF ALL THOSE VALUABLE PERSONNEL?
GIRI (PRESS)
WHERE SHOULD I HURT YOU NEXT, I WONDER?
YOUR RIGHT ARM, MAYBE? YOUR LEG!?
OR PERHAPS YOUR EYE!!!
AH...
ZAAA (WHOOSH)
WHAT ARE YOU BABBLING ABOUT—
GURA (SLUMP)
ONCE AGAIN...
...YOU'VE COME TO SAVE ME.

AH...
AAAAAAH!!
MY LEG... MY LEG!!!
BUT HOW!!? YOU RAN OUT OF MAGIC AGES AGO!!!
TCH...THEY DON'T CALL ME THE GALE FOR NOTHING, YOU KNOW!!
ONE LEG IS MORE THAN ENOUGH TO FINISH YOU OFF!!!
HYUO (SWOOSH)
WHAT A FOOL.

YOU'VE STEPPED ...
...RIGHT INTO HIS RANGE.

DO
(DOOSH)

OHHH...
IT'S BEEN TOO LONG...
DOSHA (WHUMP)
...MASTER SHADOW ...!!!

......
...EXPLAIN YOURSELF.
WHAT IN THE WORLD HAPPENED HERE?
HER NAME WAS... VICTORIA, RIGHT...?
THE FRAIL GIRL WITH THE POSSESSION I FOUND WHEN I WAS OUT TAKING A WALK LAST YEAR.
WHAT'S SHE DOING ALL COVERED IN BLOOD?
THE CULT SET YET ANOTHER OF THEIR PLANS INTO MOTION.
THAT WAS WHEN I MADE A SMALL BLUNDER...
A BLUNDER, HUH?
AHA...SO, LIKE, SHE WAS DOING SOMETHING NAUGHTY, AND THE SOLDIERS CAUGHT HER?
TRYING TO COVER IT UP WITH THAT MADE-UP STORY ABOUT THE CULT IS A CLASSIC SHADOW GARDEN MOVE!!

MY DEEPEST APOLOGIES, MY LORD.
THE FACT IS...
...WE HAVE A TRAITOR IN THE SHADOW GARDEN.
OOO (VWOO)
GUSHA (SPLURT)
A TRAITOR...
...YOU SAY!!?
end

To be continued in *The Eminence in Shadow*, Vol. 11

Art
Anri Sakano
Original Story
Daisuke Aizawa
Character Design
Touzai

The Eminence in Shadow 10

LETTERING: Jamil Stewart

TRANSLATION: Nathaniel Hiroshi Thrasher

Yen Press
150 West 30th Street
19th Floor
New York, NY 10001

Visit us at yenpress.com
facebook.com/yenpress
twitter.com/yenpress
yenpress.tumblr.com
instagram.com/yenpress

First Yen Press Edition: July 2024
Edited by Yen Press Editorial: Thomas McAlister, Carl Li
Designed by Yen Press Design: Wendy Chan

Yen Press is an imprint of Yen Press, LLC.
The Yen Press name and logo are trademarks of Yen Press, LLC.

The publisher is not responsible for websites (or their content) that are not owned by the publisher.

Library of Congress Control Number: 2021935892

ISBNs: 978-1-9753-7685-7 (paperback)
978-1-9753-7686-4 (ebook)

10 9 8 7 6 5 4 3 2 1

WOR

Printed in the United States of America